Let's Go to the Market

Come on, let's go,
come on, let's go,
come on, let's go to the market.

We're going to buy some healthy food.
We're going to buy some vegetables.

Fill the basket up with

lettuce, celery, broccoli, zucchini,
tomatoes, potatoes, carrots, and corn.

3

Come on, let's go,
come on, let's go,
come on, let's go to the market.

4

We're going to buy some healthy food.
We're going to buy some grains.

Fill the basket up with

wheat bread, bagels, crackers, tortillas, pasta, granola, oatmeal, and rice.

Come on, let's go,
come on, let's go,
come on, let's go to the market.

We're going to buy some healthy food.
We're going to buy some fruit.

Fill the basket up with

apples, strawberries, grapefruit, bananas, peaches, nectarines, watermelon, and grapes.

Come on, let's go,
come on, let's go,
come on, let's go to the market.

We're going to buy some healthy food.
We're going to buy some protein.

Fill the basket up with

chicken, soybeans, hamburger, cottage cheese, yogurt, fresh fish, peanut butter, and eggs.

Come on, let's go,
come on, let's go,
come on, let's go to the market.

We're going to buy some healthy food.
We're going to buy what's good to eat.